Illustrated by Rowan Clifford

PUFFIN

PUFFIN BOOKS

UK | USA | Canada | Ireland | Australia
India | New Zealand | South Africa

Puffin Books is part of the Penguin Random House group of companies
whose addresses can be found at global.penguinrandomhouse.com.

www.penguin.co.uk
www.puffin.co.uk
www.ladybird.co.uk

Penguin Random House UK

First published 2017
001

Typeset in Baskerville MT by Mandy Norman
Printed in Great Britain by Clays Ltd, St Ives plc

A CIP catalogue record for this book is available from the British Library

ISBN: 978-0-141-38542-6

All correspondence to:
Puffin Books
Penguin Random House Children's
80 Strand, London, WC2R 0RL

My family [illegible] off on holiday . . .

But I don't think it's going to be very relaxing . . .

ARE YOU FEELING SILLY ENOUGH TO READ MORE?

My Brother's Famous Bottom

MY DAD'S GOT AN ALLIGATOR!
MY GRANNY'S GREAT ESCAPE
MY MUM'S GOING TO EXPLODE!
MY BROTHER'S FAMOUS BOTTOM
MY BROTHER'S FAMOUS BOTTOM GETS PINCHED
MY BROTHER'S FAMOUS BOTTOM GOES CAMPING
MY BROTHER'S HOT CROSS BOTTOM
MY BROTHER'S CHRISTMAS BOTTOM – UNWRAPPED!
MY BROTHER'S FAMOUS BOTTOM GETS CROWNED!
MY BROTHER'S FAMOUS BOTTOM TAKES OFF!
MY BROTHER'S FAMOUS BOTTOM MAKES A SPLASH

The Hundred-mile-an-hour Dog

THE HUNDRED-MILE-AN-HOUR DOG
RETURN OF THE HUNDRED-MILE-AN-HOUR DOG
CHRISTMAS CHAOS FOR THE HUNDRED-MILE-AN-HOUR DOG
WANTED! THE HUNDRED-MILE-AN-HOUR DOG
LOST! THE HUNDRED-MILE-AN-HOUR DOG
THE HUNDRED-MILE-AN-HOUR DOG GOES FOR GOLD!
KIDNAPPED! THE HUNDRED-MILE-AN-HOUR DOG'S SIZZLING SUMMER
THE HUNDRED-MILE-AN-HOUR DOG: MASTER OF DISGUISE

Cartoon Kid

CARTOON KID – SUPERCHARGED!
CARTOON KID STRIKES BACK!
CARTOON KID – EMERGENCY!
CARTOON KID – ZOMBIES!

Romans on the Rampage

ROMANS ON THE RAMPAGE
ROMANS ON THE RAMPAGE: JAIL BREAK!
ROMANS ON THE RAMPAGE: CHARIOT CHAMPIONS!

AND EVEN MORE?

THE BEAK SPEAKS
BEWARE! KILLER TOMATOES
FATBAG: THE DEMON VACUUM CLEANER
INVASION OF THE CHRISTMAS PUDDINGS

JEREMY STRONG'S LAUGH-YOUR-SOCKS-OFF JOKE BOOK
JEREMY STRONG'S LAUGH-YOUR-SOCKS-OFF EVEN MORE JOKE BOOK

This story is for Joe and Noah.

I hope you laugh so much you fall out of bed.

Contents

1. Watch Out, Dad's About!

My dad's been arrested! He really has. He's always doing daft things and getting into a mess. This time he was put in a police van and taken to the police station by two policemen, one policewoman and three park keepers. I was nearly put in the van with him! There had been a problem at the park. This is what happened.

A few days ago Dad came home with an extra-large cardboard box. It was very long, not very wide and even thinner. Guess what was inside? A paddleboard. Paddleboards are a bit like surfboards but you paddle them. (Duh! Of course!) They are A.W.E.S.O.M.E.

'Want a go!' shouted Cheese.

'Want a go!' yelled Tomato. (They are only three years old. I'm eleven.)

They both jumped on the board. Dad stood there, hands on hips, and grinned at all of us.

The way he was grinning, he looked rather like a three-year-old himself, with a beard. 'Isn't it brilliant?'

Mum watched them with her arms folded across her chest. That's what she does when she can see a problem coming, or even several problems.

'Ron, do you know how to paddleboard?'

'Of course. You stand on it and use the paddle. Ta da! That's why they are called paddleboards. It's a board that you paddle. Ta da! Ta da!'

Mum took a deep breath. 'Even I have managed to work that out,' she said stonily. 'But there's one thing missing. Water. The sea. The board will be floating on water and you will have to stay on the board and not fall off and drown.'

'I know that,' said Dad. 'Do I look like a numbnut?'

'No, you don't,' agreed Mum. 'You just behave like a numbnut. Quite often. Most of the time, in fact.'

'Thank you very much,' Dad shot back.

'You're welcome,' said Mum with a smile. 'I suppose you are planning to take that on holiday next week.'

'Exactly. What is more, I shall do lots of practice before we go, so by the time we set off I shall be an expert.'

'That board won't fit in the bath,' Mum pointed out.

'Ha! I shan't practise in the bath. I'm going to take the board down to the park and practise on the pond. Ta da – again!'

Mum's eyes almost jumped out of her face. 'Are you crazy?'

Dad drew himself up and tried to look as un-crazy as he possibly could. 'No, I am not. I need somewhere to practise and the park pond is safe and quiet.'

Mum turned to me. 'Nicholas, please tell your father that he can't paddleboard on the park pond. I'm sure it's forbidden. They have rules there, you know.'

'It's true, Dad,' I said. 'There's a big notice that says PLEASE DON'T FEED BREAD TO THE DUCKS. IT IS BAD FOR THEM and another one that says NO SWIMMING, DIVING OR PADDLING.'

Dad gave us a crafty smile. 'Is there a notice that says NO *PADDLEBOARDING*?'

I shook my head. Mum shook her head. The twins shook their heads.

'Good,' said Dad. 'That's where I shall go and practise, then.'

And he did. Then he got arrested.

He didn't get arrested straight away. Several things happened first.

He put on his wet suit and took the paddleboard to the park. Do you remember I told you how long a paddleboard is? He did look a little odd as he plodded down to the park in his wet suit, mask and snorkel, carrying the board. I was with him and I can tell you that we got a lot of strange looks from passers-by.

When we got to the park we found several

people already there, mostly mothers and small children. They were feeding the ducks. (*Not* with bread, obviously.)

So Dad got his paddleboard and walked to the edge of the lake. He swung the board round to put it on the water. Unfortunately, as the board whizzed round it hit a small girl and sent her flying into the pond. I did try to warn Dad but it was too late.

The girl screamed.

All the mothers yelled and one of them rushed in to grab the victim. Dad was confused and upset. He tried to un-swing the paddleboard and this time he whacked a mother into the water. She crashed into the first mother, who was just rescuing her soaking child, and all three of them fell back into the pond. Everyone started screaming again.

'Stop! Stop!'

Two park keepers hurried over, shouting at Dad. 'No paddleboarding on the pond!'

'It doesn't say that anywhere!' Dad yelled back. He turned to the mothers and children, this time smacking one of the park keepers into the water with a resounding splash.

'Sorry, so sorry. This board is a bit difficult to handle. Oh dear!' cried Dad, swinging the board back the other way and hurling the other park keeper in to join the first one. I was hopping about from one foot to the other trying to warn Dad, not to mention anyone anywhere near him.

As Dad explained to Mum later, the problem was that if he watched the front of the board, he couldn't see what the back was doing, and if he looked at the back of the board, he couldn't see what the front was doing.

I heard a distant siren. It was closing in on the park, getting louder and louder. One of the mums had called the police. Well, to cut short a *very* long, noisy and exceedingly splashy story, one policewoman plus Sergeant Smugg and another child, along with two mothers and one of the park keepers who had already been well soaked, *all* went smack back into the pond. As for the ducks, they had long since departed to the far corner, where they sat laughing at the clown show taking place.

Dad tried to explain everything to the increasingly wet crowd around him. 'We're going on holiday next week!' he moaned. 'I just wanted to practise my paddleboarding.'

'You're a danger to shipping!' cursed a sodden park keeper. 'You should be locked up.'

And Dad *was* locked up. It was only for half an hour or so. I don't think even Sergeant Smugg wanted to put Dad in jail, but they did want to keep the police station safe from giant paddleboards knocking everyone flying. The paddleboard had been arrested too.

Sergeant Smugg even wanted to arrest me, but Dad told him I was an innocent by-stander, not a major criminal. I had to run home and tell Mum and she had to go and rescue him.

'Daddy's a climmerlim,' Tomato announced.

'Criminal,' corrected Mum, glaring at Dad.

'Bad Daddy,' Cheese added for good measure.

'Bad Daddy,' echoed Tomato.

Dad looked glumly at all of us. 'I didn't mean any harm,' he said.

'You never *mean* it,' Mum pointed out. 'It just happens, Ron. And it only happens to you. Only you could take a paddleboard outside and almost drown nine strangers within minutes of leaving the house.'

Dad suddenly brightened. 'Nine? As many as that? Is that a record? Maybe I should contact *The Big Book of Records* people and get my name in the book.'

But before Dad could get out his mobile, Sergeant Smugg came across, waving the keys to Dad's cell.

'I can only let you out,' the sergeant said, 'when

you have paid for the dry cleaning of two park keepers' uniforms, three policemen's uniforms, four sun dresses and five assorted items of children's clothing. That would come to £175.00.'

Dad gulped, his lips moving silently as he repeated the figure to himself. He handed over his bank card. It went through the machine and Sergeant Smugg opened the cell door.

'You can go now,' he said. 'Have a nice holiday. Please take your paddleboard with you. I suggest you leave it wherever it is that you're going.'

'Turkey,' muttered Dad.

Sergeant Smugg gave a grim smile. 'Right. Turkey, eh? I'll phone ahead and warn them that you're coming.'

2. Really Gigantic Strawberries and an Awful Lot of Teeth

Mum suggested that we should make a list of the things we wanted to take to Turkey. 'Make a note of any special clothes and other items you might want,' she said. 'And don't forget your swimming costumes. Nicholas, you can help the twins.'

Well, I did help the twins with their lists and this is what I wrote down for them:

- Teddy Bear (for Cheese) and Big Polar Bear (for Tomato. It's even bigger than her.)
- Lego collection (about eight crates of Lego)
- Tricycle (one each)
- Trampoline
- Tunnel (it's one of those crawl-through things)
- Plastic slide (for the end of the tunnel)

• Scissors, crayons, glue, sprinkly stuff and those things that go bang in crackers
• Schumacher (he's our tortoise); Captain Beaky and all our hens; Rubbish (our goat)
• Superman costume (for Tomato); Tyrannosaurus Rex costume (for Cheese)
• ~~Five~~ Six hundred bars of chocolate (for Cheese)
• Clear plastic box with lid (to put a dolphin in to bring back home, for both of them)

I showed it to Mum. She gave it straight back to me. 'Fine. Now go and do a proper one. It's bad enough to have one numbnut in the family. Please don't encourage the twins.'

Both the twins burst into tears.

'Poo!' shouted Tomato. 'Horrible Mummy!'

'Poo poo poo poo POO!' yelled Cheese. (Sorry. That's Cheese's favourite word. He is only three.)

'You only have a small case,' Mum explained patiently. 'You can't take big things and you certainly can't take animals.'

'That's poo!' said Cheese, pouting his lower lip.

Tomato sniffed. 'But they'll die. Nobody will feed them. We shall come home and find deaded chickens and a deaded tortoise and a deaded Rubbish and a deaded everything.' She sniffed even more noisily.

'Nothing is going to die while we are away,' said Mum. 'Granny and Lancelot are going to come and live in our house while we are on holiday. They will look after all the animals.'

Tomato stared at Mum for a moment. She wasn't going to give up and she shook her head. 'Granny will be deaded and Lancelot will be deaded and his motorbike will be deaded.'

'Stop being silly. Of course they won't. They'll be fine. Granny and Lancelot will feed the animals.'

Mum bent down and wiped the tears from their cheeks. 'Now, will it help if I give each of you one of those really gigantically enormous strawberries from the fridge? Will that make things better?'

The strawberries did, and the twins quickly forgot all about Granny and her husband, so that was all right and they went off to pack their suitcases. Fortunately Dad went to check their bags before we actually left for the airport. He stared, astonished, at the open cases. The clothes were heaped in piles and they were moving around as if they were alive.

'What on earth?' muttered Dad, gingerly

taking hold of the corner of a wriggling jumper. He whipped it away.

'Argh!' He leaped back as a hen poked up its head and snapped at his hand.

'Didn't your mother say *no* animals on the plane? What else have you got in there? More hens? Bouncing bananas! You have! *All of them!* And what's that under your swimming costume? Schumacher! You can't take hens and tortoises on aeroplanes! Now help me get them back outside.'

'They'll be lonely,' muttered Tomato.

'No, they won't. Granny and Lancelot will read them bedtime stories every night. Take them back outside.'

At last we seemed to have everything sorted and we actually managed to set off for the airport. Exciting! Next stop Turkey!

EXCEPT –

– we almost never got there at all.

BECAUSE –

– we almost missed the plane.

BECAUSE –

– there was a bit of a problem at the airport. Everything was fine until we got there, but then Dad's paddleboard went berserk. It really did seem to have a life of its own. It was OK at first because Dad stood it upright while we waited in the queue to check in for our flight. At last we got to the desk, where a woman with very red lipstick, a big smile and what looked like far too many teeth was waiting.

'Can I see your passports, please, and your booking?'

Dad turned to Mum. 'You've got them, haven't you?'

'I gave them to you,' said Mum. 'Remember? You said you wanted to keep them all together.'

'Oh, yes!' said Dad, beaming at the lady behind the desk. 'Silly me. I've got them.'

Dad began rummaging around in his pockets but it was difficult because he was still trying to hold on to the paddleboard.

'Let me hold it,' suggested Mum.

'I can manage,' snapped Dad, as the paddleboard slipped to the side and almost clouted the woman waiting behind Dad.

'Watch out!' she cried, ducking to avoid having her head knocked off.

'I am watching out,' growled Dad. 'That's the problem.'

'Can I have your passports, please?' the lady asked again, still smiling.

'I'm getting them. Just a second –' Dad

changed hands and the paddleboard started swinging about.

'Ow!' cried an old man in a wheelchair as Dad clunked him on the head.

'For heaven's sake!' shouted the woman as the paddleboard knocked over her suitcase and the contents spilled across the floor. The paddleboard was now swinging about with several bits of the woman's clothing hanging from it.

'Can't you control that thing, you idiot?' someone else demanded.

'It's the paddleboard that's an idiot!' Dad shouted back. 'Not me!'

'Passports, please!' the desk lady repeated for the third time, her smile getting rather impatient.

I could see this could go on forever, so I just grabbed the paddleboard myself and yanked it from Dad's grasp. I stuck it upright and held on to it tightly.

Dad began to breathe more easily. 'Thank you, Nicholas. That's a great help.'

'Your son is a lot more use than you are,' someone in the queue muttered.

'And he's a lot more polite than you are!' Dad snapped back, pulling out the passports at last and handing them to the lady. She checked them and very wisely said that the paddleboard would have to go in the hold of the aircraft.

'Do you have any unusual objects in your bags?' she asked.

'I've got a hen,' Tomato piped up.

'Really?' The lady's eyes doubled in size.

Tomato nodded.

'No, you haven't,' said Mum. 'You unpacked the hen, remember?' Mum looked carefully at Tomato. 'You *did* take Mavis Moppet out of your suitcase, didn't you?'

Tomato pressed her lips together very tightly. Mum tried to smile at the lady on the desk. 'I'm sure she took the hen out.'

'You mean there was a *real* hen in there? Not a toy one?'

'Oh, for heaven's sake!' yelled the man in the wheelchair. 'First of all it's a gigantic paddleboard and now there's a hen in the girl's case! The whole family's bonkers!'

'Keep your opinions to yourself,' Mum said coldly. 'Huh! Think we're bonkers, do you? You haven't seen anything yet. This is what we're like on a good day.'

The lady stamped our boarding cards and handed them over the counter.

'Enjoy your holiday,' she said, giving us a big red-and-bright-white smile.

'You have very nice teeth,' Dad told her. 'And an awful lot of them.'

The lady blushed and looked rather alarmed.

'Just ignore him,' Mum advised. 'I do.'

At last we were all checked in and it wasn't long before we were sitting on the plane and on our way. HOORAY!

3. Ice Cream and Pumpkin Pie

TURKEY – it's hot! The sand burns your feet! I have to keep my flip-flops on and even then the sand gets in at the sides and I end up hopping about from one bit of shade to the next. Quick, jump in the sea and cool down. Ahhhh, lovely!

You can imagine what it's like when all five of us are on the beach – four people going 'Ooh! Ow! Ouch! Eeek!' and hop-popping about like a bunch of noisy twits on pogo sticks. Mum, of course, wears sensible trainers and just watches us with an amused smile.

Dad's bought some new sunglasses. 'They are so cool,' he said, leaning casually against his propped-up paddleboard. 'Do I look like a film star?'

'No,' Mum answered.

'How about a guy from a rock band?'

Mum shook her head.

Dad frowned. 'You're just trying to annoy me,' he said.

'Yes.' Mum peered over her own sunglasses and flashed a smile at him. 'I am, because I don't care if you look cool, or like a film star, or a boy from a band. I love you just the way you are.' And she blew Dad a kiss.

Dad went to blow a kiss back but the paddleboard suddenly slipped and all he managed to do was collapse on the burning

sand and then leap up, yelling. 'I'm on fire!' he bellowed as he went crashing off into the sea to cool down.

Mum watched for a moment, waved and called after him, 'Now you look cool!'

A family sitting near us on the beach looked across at Mum. The woman had a sharp, thin nose and her eyes were close together so she looked a bit like a bird – a heron maybe, or a stork. Anyhow, she was sitting up on her sunbed watching Dad's theatrics.

'Is your husband always as noisy as this?' she asked.

'Noisy?' repeated Mum. 'Not at all. You wait until he really gets going. You won't be able to hear yourself breathe.' Mum turned her attention back to her magazine, leaving the woman boggle-eyed and lost for words.

Her name is Mrs Grubnose. She and her husband have got a son, Mason. His nose is just like his mother's, and his eyes too. Mason has a

way of looking at you as if he'd like to push you into a giant liquidizer and press the start button.

Mr Grubnose is something else. He is short and thin and has a moustache that looks as if it has been sneezed out of his nose and then got stuck on his upper lip. His swimming shorts are ridiculously baggy and his tiny legs poke out like a pair of twigs. In other words the whole family is *weird*. I shall certainly try and keep well clear of Mason.

But apart from the Grubnoses everything is *super-brilliant*! You should have seen breakfast this morning. The table was piled high with fabulous food. The twins were so excited they had to show everyone.

'Look! CHEESE!' shouted Cheese.

'TOMATO!' shouted Tomato. They looked at each other, picked up their food and waved it wildly at everyone in the restaurant.

'CHEESE AND TOMATO!' they yelled. The whole restaurant stared. Mum turned to Dad.

'You're the one who decided to call the twins Cheese and Tomato, so I shall let you explain why they're so excited.'

Dad turned red and gazed at the sea of faces looking questioningly at us. 'Um, I think I left something upstairs in our room,' he said and quickly left.

'Coward!' Mum called after him, and she winked at me, then turned to the twins. 'Now then, you two, put that food down and stop making such an exhibition of yourselves.'

The Grubnoses were seated a couple of tables away but while most of the restaurant was chuckling and pointing, all three Grubnoses were scowling like a bunch of giraffes trying to put on pyjamas. Oh, well, you can't please everyone.

Anyhow, breakfast was brilliant and Hotel Kismet is brilliant and we've got fabulous rooms. Mum and Dad have a room and the twins and I have a room opposite theirs. *Plus*, both rooms have balconies where we can sit and look at the sea or the people down below in the street going shopping.

It's fantastic, except when Tomato decided to get rid of the rest of the apple she didn't want and threw it over the balcony and almost hit Mrs Grubnose, who was trying on some earrings outside a shop. She looked up but we ducked down very quickly and I don't think she saw us.

The little town we are in is called Kalkan and it's pretty, especially by the harbour. There are loads of animals on the streets. Well, maybe not loads, but there are quite a few cats and dogs wandering about. Irfan and the hotel manager Arif say that the animals don't belong to anyone and have no homes, which is pretty sad. Irfan works on Reception and also he's the waiter at our table. He knows everything and speaks very good English –

and even better Turkish. In fact, I said to him, completely deadpan: 'You speak brilliant Turkish, Irfan.'

He frowned and searched my face. Was I serious? Then his shoulders began to heave with laughter. 'Yes! Very good Turkish. I speak very, *very* good Turkish. Maybe I *am* Turkish! You are funny man, Nicky, like your *baba*, father.'

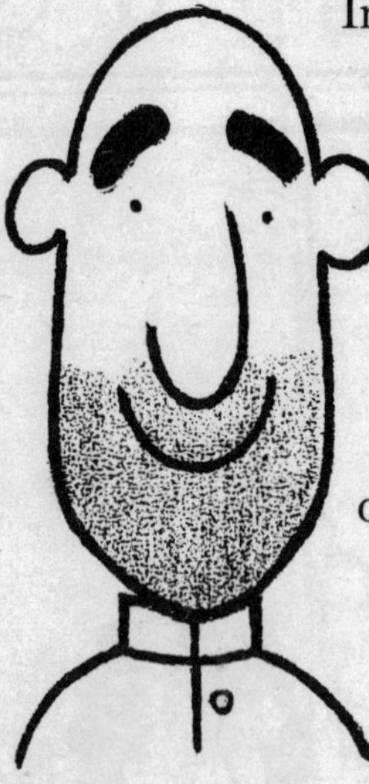

Irfan's name sounds like 'ear-fan' when you say it, which is really funny because it's as if Irfan has huge ears that he can flap about like fans. He hasn't and he can't. His ears are actually quite neat and small. He is good looking and has very twinkly eyes.

The twins like all the animals. They want to stroke all the cats and pat all the dogs and I think they would like to take all of them home with them.

'Can we have a dog in our room?' Tomato asked Mum and Dad.

'No.'

'Can we have a cat?' Cheese wanted to know.

'No.'

'A very small cat?'

'No.'

'Why not?' Tomato demanded.

'Because this is a hotel for people,' Dad explained.

'Can we go to an animal hotel?' Tomato piped up.

'No, we can't, because we're people. The animals won't let us in,' Dad added.

Cheese sniffed. 'When I grow up I shall have a hotel for animals *and* people.'

'Like a zoo,' Tomato added. 'With people in cages. Daddy in a cage. Mummy in a cage.'

'That's not very nice,' said Mum. 'I don't want to be in a cage. Anyhow, you're talking nonsense. Let's go to the beach.'

'BEACH!' yelled Cheese.

So we went down to the beach. On the way we had to stop about two hundred times to say hello to various cats and dogs. One of the dogs just would not stop following us. It had a rather cute face, rough, sandy-coloured hair and one ear up and one ear down. The 'up' ear had a little blue plastic ring attached to it.

'I wonder what his name is?' said Mum.

'I think it's a girl dog,' I told her.

'Poobum,' said Cheese. Mum eyed him sharply.

'That's rude and not nice. You can't call a dog Poobum. Think again.'

Cheese thought again and suddenly smiled. 'Bumpoo!'

'No!' cried Mum, half laughing. 'That's just as bad as before. Think of something nice.'

'Ice Cream,' Tomato shouted. 'It's a girl dog. Nicky says so and her name is Ice Cream.'

Mum groaned and scratched her head. What was she to say? It wasn't rude. It was nice.

'You can't call a dog Ice Cream,' Dad said.

'Why ever not?' asked Mum. 'You called the twins Cheese and Tomato, which is a lot more daft than calling a dog Ice Cream. I think it's a very good name.'

At the beach Ice Cream came and sat beside us and wagged her tail in the sand.

The Grubnoses were lying on the same sunbeds as before. They eyed us crossly.

'Dogs shouldn't be allowed on beaches,' said Mrs Grubnose.

Dad shrugged, glanced at Ice Cream and then looked back at Mrs Grubnose.

'You'll have to tell the dog, then. She only understands Turkish. Besides, she doesn't belong to us.'

Mrs Grubnose's eyes narrowed angrily. She gave a huff and turned her back on us. Mason looked at me very hard, pointed at Ice Cream and made his hand into a gun shape. What a charming boy.

Dad gazed out to sea. Several boats were slowly sailing from one little island to another, looking for bays. When they stopped everyone would swim in the sea for a bit. Then they would climb back on board and set off for another island, a new bay and more swimming.

Dad's eyes had gone all dreamy and thoughtful. 'Tomorrow,' he announced, 'I am going to paddle to that little island out there.'

'Daddy going for a PIDDLE!' shouted Cheese, and suddenly half the beach was looking at us.

Dad had gone very red. He got to his feet. 'He means "paddle". I'm going paddleboarding tomorrow. Cheese gets his words mixed up. Sorry.'

Mr Grubnose choked. 'You call your son "Cheese"? What kind of grown man calls his own son "Cheese"?'

'This kind of grown man.' Dad smiled, poking his own chest. 'And he calls his daughter "Tomato" and his wife "Pumpkin Pie" – and it's none of your business. Bye-bye.' And he sat down.

Mum glared at him. 'You have never, ever called me Pumpkin Pie,' she hissed.

'It's never too late to start, Pumpkin,' chuckled Dad.

'*Don't you dare!*' But Mum couldn't help laughing herself. She settled back on her sunbed, with one hand scratching Ice Cream's head as the dog lay on the sand beside her.

4. Captain Disaster

We spent the rest of the day checking out our new surroundings. Guess what? We found shops where you could hire paddleboards. Dad needn't have brought his paddleboard on the plane after all. And we wouldn't have had all that fuss at the airport!

I could tell by the look on her face that Mum was not impressed. However, she didn't say a word. Neither did Dad! But I could tell by the look on *his* face that he knew what Mum was thinking and *she* knew that *he* knew. I think that being an adult must be very complicated sometimes.

Ice Cream followed us all the way back to the hotel and wanted to come inside. We could tell this by the way she pawed at the front door

and looked at us with very shiny, hopeful eyes. Cheese and Tomato were pretty upset when Mum and Dad both said it wasn't possible.

'But if it rains she'll get wet,' snivelled Tomato.

'We're in Turkey. It doesn't rain here in the summer. That's why we came,' Mum said, drily. 'Besides, there are plenty of places outside where she can shelter if it does rain.'

'She'll be hungry,' said Cheese. 'She'll starve and then she'll be deaded.'

Tomato gave another sniff. 'I don't like deaded dogs.'

'I have never seen such a well-fed dog,' Dad told the twins. 'Her stomach is bulging. She's probably eaten at least six meals today already.'

It was my turn to speak up. 'I asked Irfan why some of the dogs and cats have got blue plastic earrings in one ear. He said it was to show that they had been neutered and were being looked after by an animal charity. The charity puts food out for them too.'

'Ah! I wondered why most of the strays seemed to be well fed and looked after. Good for them.' Dad nodded.

The twins cheered up when they heard about the charity and we were able to go into the hotel and leave Ice Cream outside. So that was all right, at least for now.

The next day was paddleboarding day and Dad was true to his word. We had hardly got breakfast out of the way – cheese, bread, four different jams, eggs, olives, tomatoes, cucumber, pastries, melon, grapes, figs – when Dad shot off to get the board from their room. It was time for the beach.

'Are you really going to do this?' asked Mum, as we stood on the beach and watched Dad prepare for his trip. 'I mean, I know you have lots of daft ideas but paddling to that island must be the most seriously *bad* idea ever.'

'Nonsense. That island is hardly any distance at all. I could almost walk there and besides, paddleboards don't sink.'

Mum gave Dad a hard look. 'Maybe paddleboards don't, but humans do.'

Dad held up a yellow life jacket. 'I shall be wearing this.'

'OK, so maybe you won't sink, but that island is still a long way off and you do have a habit of getting into trouble, Ron. Things go wrong. Don't ask me why. Sometimes I think you should really be called Captain Disaster.'

'Huh – very funny,' Dad mumbled grumpily as he pulled on the life jacket. 'Right, I'm ready.' He edged towards the water.

'How will we know when you get there?' I asked.

'I've got my mobile in a waterproof bag. I'll text you. Byeeee!'

And with that Dad climbed on to the paddleboard and set off. When you're paddling the board, you start off kneeling down and then slowly get to your feet. Dad only fell off five times when he tried to stand up. And that was barely three metres from the beach.

Mum shouted at him, 'Captain Disaster!'

Dad yelled something back but we didn't quite catch what he said, which was probably a good thing. In any case, it wasn't long before we lost sight of him and had to stop looking.

'Anyone for an ice cream?' suggested Mum cheerfully. The twins had hardly stopped yelling 'YES!' when a quite different kind of Ice Cream was right next to us, wagging her tail furiously.

'Ice Cream wants an ice cream!' Tomato laughed.

'Yes. I can see that,' said Mum. 'What kind of ice cream do you think our Ice Cream dog is? Chocolate? Mint?'

'Toffee,' said Cheese. 'Because she's toffee-coloured. She's Toffee Ice Cream.'

'That's a very long name for a dog,' Mum observed.

We got our ices and the dog immediately ate Cheese's before he'd managed a single lick. You have never seen such a sad face.

'Bad dog! Poo dog!' Cheese scolded. 'Don't like you any more!'

'You can't blame the dog,' Mum said. 'That's what most dogs will do if you give them the chance. Nicky, here's some money. Go and get another ice cream, and make sure Cheese gets it this time.'

I went off and joined the ice-cream queue. I was looking around while I was waiting. Things were getting very busy in the bay. Boats and jet skis were whizzing about, all heading in the same direction, towards the nearest island. Something odd was going on. My stomach gave a horrible lurch, my heart stopped beating and when it started up again it was going twice as fast.

CAPTAIN DISASTER!!!

I ran like mad back to the others. Everyone on the beach was on their feet, staring out to sea. Mum was holding her mobile to her ear and – talking.

'Where are you? – What do you mean, you're "in the sea". The sea is a big place, Ron. Are you *in* the sea or *on* it? – What? A bit of both? Some bits of you are in the sea and some are on it? What does that mean? Are you in bits, floating about? – Yes, of course I'm joking! – Your life jacket came off? How did that happen? – It was rubbing you under your arms? Oh, you poor little baby, I don't think! You great, crumbling cabbage-head! Well, you're obviously not drowning if you're able to ring me, so what's going on? There are about fifty boats out there looking – Oh, they've found you? Good. – One of them is going to tow you back? – Yes, of course we'll wait here. Honestly, you are such an embarrassment. Put your life jacket on and get back here. Goodbye.'

Mum put her phone in her bag and folded her arms. She looked at me.

'Nicholas, I want you to know that fathers are meant to be good role models for their sons to copy. However, your father is providing you with an excellent example of a role model that you should *not* copy at any time whatsoever. I hope you understand that.'

I nodded. 'Captain Disaster?' I hinted.

'Yes. Indeed. Captain Disaster and God of Calamities, Catastrophes,

Mishaps, Mayhem and Accidents. Have I missed anything out?'

I shook my head. We both watched as a jet ski approached the shore, towing Dad to safety on his paddleboard. As soon as he caught sight of us Dad stood up, waved cheerfully and promptly fell into the sea. The jet-skier didn't notice and carried on towing the empty board. Dad had to swim the final twenty metres to the shore.

He waded slowly out of the water, collected the paddleboard, shook hands

with the jet-skier and came across to us.

'Phew!' he said. 'That was an adventure.'

'No, Ron, it was *not* an adventure. It was an embarrassment. The entire town of Kalkan now knows that I have an idiot for a husband. I am banning you from using your paddleboard for the rest of this holiday. Furthermore, you are *not* taking it back home on the plane. I refuse to go through all that fuss at the airport again.'

'But what about my paddleboard?' asked Dad.

'It can be chopped up for firewood, for all I care,' declared Mum.

'That's a bit harsh,' said Dad, pulling at his beard.

'Maybe,' Mum told him. 'But if it means that you will be safer then I shall feel a lot happier because, you see, despite the fact that you are a crumbling cabbage-head, I still happen to love you and care for you and I would rather you didn't drown. Now, go and get Cheese and yourself an ice cream like a good little boy. And don't let Ice Cream eat it. She's already had Cheese's first one!'

We sat down on the beach. Dad came back and things quietened down. Mum handed me a postcard and said I should write to Granny and Lancelot, so I did.

Dear Granny and Lancelot,
We are having brilliant fun. Dad went on his paddleboard and had to be rescued by fifty boats and jet skis. There is a dog called Ice Cream and she follows us everywhere. She is lovely. Cheese and Tomato want to keep her. They will probably smuggle her on to the plane!
Love from Nicholas. XX

5. Three Lobsters and a Bumpy Problem

When we went down for breakfast this morning the whole room fell silent as all the other guests stopped eating and stared at us. Some of them grinned. One woman winked at me! (Or maybe she was winking at Dad.)

Then they all went back to their breakfast eating, all except the Grubnoses, who looked as if they'd had a bath in a giant tub of tomato soup, because they had spent far too much time in the sun the day before. Mrs Grubnose slowly looked around the room and then spoke to her husband and son in a voice loud enough to reach the boats in the harbour.

'Did you hear about that silly, silly man who went to sea on his paddleboard and had to be rescued? A paddleboard! Can you imagine doing anything so stupid? It's unbelievable how brainless some people can be. If he were my husband I think I'd have to get a divorce at once!'

It was *so* embarrassing. Dad flushed scarlet and was trying to hide behind his beard, but Mum didn't seem to mind. She lifted her chin and spoke to Dad in a voice even louder than Mrs Grubnose's.

'Darling, did you see that extraordinary family who lay in the sun all day yesterday? Can you imagine anything so stupid? Now they are so red they look like three boiled lobsters!'

A ripple of laughter ran round the room while the three lobsters turned even redder than their sunburn and shrivelled in their seats.

'Lying in the sun, all day,' Mum went on. 'You'd think they'd be intelligent enough to realize how dangerous that can be. Oh, well, let's hope they've got a good stock of after-sun lotion to put on. They'll probably need to bath in it. Now then, what shall we do today? I think we should all get on the paddleboard and go out to sea together. I'm sure that with five of us paddling we can get to that island. Come on!'

And with that Mum got up from the table and we followed her out. Behind us, several people clapped. I even heard someone shout, 'Encore!'

Outside the breakfast room I hurried after Mum. I couldn't believe what she'd said. 'Are we really going on the paddleboard? Five of us? Won't it sink?'

Mum chuckled. 'Of course we're not, Nicholas. I only said all that to annoy the

Grubnoses. There is no way you will get me on a paddleboard, surfboard, skateboard or ironing board for that matter!'

Dad put one arm around Mum's shoulders and hugged her. 'That was wonderful. You really nobbled the Grubnoses. I shan't be able to stop thinking of them as lobsters now.'

'Yes, well, don't get too excited, Ron. You can stop being Captain Disaster, please. Let's do something a bit quieter today. Maybe we can go and look at one of the nearby ruins.'

'What sort of ruins?' I asked. It didn't sound very interesting to me.

'Your mother means old buildings,' muttered Dad, pulling his I-will-be-bored face.

'They're much more than old buildings,' Mum explained. 'They were small cities three thousand years ago. Irfan was telling me about them. The Ancient Greeks were here. The Romans were here and before either of them the Lycians were here, and they were the first to build the cities.

Irfan says we'll see wildlife too – tortoises and lizards.'

'Lizards!' repeated Tomato.

'Dinosaurs!' shouted Cheese. 'Aaaargh!' He pretended to be scared.

'I didn't say dinosaurs at all. I said lizards,' Mum corrected him. Cheese stopped running round her in circles, looked up, shouted 'Dinosaurs!' again and carried on running.

Dad nodded seriously. 'I'm with Cheese on this one. I'll be looking for dinosaurs. How about you, Nicholas?'

'Give me dinosaurs every time.' I grinned.

Mum shrugged. 'Boys will be boys,' she sighed. 'Now go and change your shoes so we can go out. Meet back here in five minutes.'

I was about to follow Cheese and Tomato up to our room when Irfan beckoned us over. 'Come see,' he whispered. We followed him towards the rear of the hotel. There was an open cupboard with lots of shelves stacked with bedding and towels, ready to use.

Irfan pointed to the bottom shelf. Nestled deep inside, so that you had to bend down to see them, were three kittens, curled up together and fast asleep.

'Oh!' whispered Tomato. 'They are beautiful.'

'Do they belong to the hotel?' I asked. Irfan shook his head.

'No home. Strays. I found them outside and brought them in here.'

'I want them,' said Tomato. Of course she did!

'I want them,' echoed Cheese, and of course he did too. So did I. They were so cute.

Irfan smiled. 'They'll be OK here. I shall keep an eye on them.'

I called to the twins. 'Come on. We've got to change our shoes. Mum will be fretting.'

We raced upstairs.

The place we went to was called Letoon and it used to be a temple but had got flooded. There were some dusty mosaics and lots of broken pillars sticking out of a big pond. There was hardly anyone there. We just about had the place to ourselves.

It was very beautiful and the pond bit was full of turtles. They sunbathed on rocks and the stumps of pillars. When you went near they would dive into the water and vanish.

Every now and then there'd be a tremendous noise and we'd hunt around, certain that there were some big birds among the reeds making all the fuss. You will never guess what it was. Tiny frogs! They were about the size of a small cupcake, but what a racket!

We also saw two kingfishers, flashing

up and down, going from one fishing spot to another, like tiny blue-and-orange fairy-spears darting through the air.

'Lizard!' Mum suddenly shouted, pointing across to a fallen pillar. It was a big one, almost half a metre long, posing on the pillar like some prehistoric monster.

'Dinosaur!' cried Cheese. 'Run, Mummy! Run, Nick! Run, Daddy!'

'What about Tomato?' I asked.

Cheese laughed. 'Dinosaur can eat Tomato!'

'That's not very nice, you little imp,' said Mum. 'Just let me catch you and I'll feed *you* to the dinosaur!'

We had a brilliant time, racing around and watching the animals. We saw three tortoises too, slowly wandering about. I love tortoises. They always look busy, but you never actually see them doing anything. It's as if their job is to plod about, like building inspectors checking on everything, stomping round and round, making notes to themselves.

'Hmmm, that rock looks all right. And that bush is growing nicely. Oooh, I don't like this lump of log across the path. I can't climb over that. I shall have to get the council to come and remove it.'

We spent half the day at Letoon and then went back to the hotel to get ready for supper. In our room Tomato pulled at my T-shirt.

'What?' I asked. She beckoned me down to her height and whispered in my ear.

'I've got a secret, Nicky,' she said.

'Really? Is it exciting? Do you want to tell me?'

'Want to show you,' Tomato said, pulling at my T-shirt again. 'Come on.'

Tomato took me into the bathroom. 'Look.'

I looked. In the bath there was a tortoise, clumsily plodding up and down, presumably wondering how on earth it was going to get out.

'But I need a plug to put in the bath,' Tomato said. 'Then I can put water in for it to swim.'

'Ah, well, this tortoise doesn't need a plug.'

'No? Why?'

'Because tortoises can't swim,' I told her.

'Yes! Yes! At The Toon, lots of tortoises in the water swimming.'

'The ones we saw swimming at Letoon weren't tortoises. They look like tortoises but they are turtles. Turtles can swim. Tortoises can't swim.'

'Oh.' Tomato looked at the tortoise in the bath and I could tell she was thinking. 'I could teach it to swim,' she suggested, hopefully.

'I don't think so. You see, they haven't got the right kind of feet. Turtles can swim because they have flippers for feet.'

'We can swim and we don't have flippers,' Tomato argued and I could see her logic.

'I know, but we have long legs and long arms

to help us. Tortoises have very short legs.'

'Mmm,' Tomato grunted, and luckily she couldn't think how to reply.

I went on: 'Anyway, the thing is, we can't keep a tortoise in the bath.'

'But I'm going to take it home!'

'You can't. This is a wild tortoise and it has to stay in this country.'

'But Bumpy needs to be looked after!'

'Bumpy?' I repeated.

'That's his name. He's called Bumpy and he's my tortoise and he knows my name and I'm taking him home.'

Tears were filling Tomato's eyes. I had to make a decision and I decided to play for time.

'Don't cry. Listen, we'll keep Bumpy here while I think of what we can do, all right? Maybe we can find some food for him. We need green leaves. I'll try and find some.'

Tomato nodded. She fetched her teddy and popped it in the bath with the tortoise.'That's so Bumpy has someone to talk to,' Tomato explained.

I smiled. All I had to do now was think of a solution to the Bumpy Problem.

6. Belly Dancing in the Rain

I was still thinking about Bumpy when Dad put his beardy head round the door and grinned at us.

'Guess what? It's karaoke night this evening.'

I groaned. I am not a karaoke fan. Unfortunately Dad loves it because he likes singing. He's always singing. Sometimes he even makes up his own songs, or rather he makes up the words. '*Twinkle, twinkle, Mr Tugg – you look like a big, bald bug. Show your face and if you do, I shall squash you under my shoe.*' That's a typical Dad song. (Mr Tugg is our Martian nightmare neighbour at home.)

'I shall serenade everyone in the hotel tonight,' crowed Dad. 'La la la LAAAAH!'

'I think I might stay in bed with a pillow over my head,' I told him.

'Nick! That's poetry! I could set it to music!' And he started singing again. '*I think I might stay in beeed, with a pillow over my heeeead!* OK, I know you don't like singing but it's not just karaoke night, there will also be – BELLY DANCING!'

Dad's eyes were wide with excitement and he began what he obviously thought was a belly dance. In fact it looked more like he had terrible pains in his stomach.

Double groan. Belly dancing *and* karaoke.

'Oh, cheer up!' said Dad. 'All you have to do is come down and watch.'

Cheese had pulled up his T-shirt and was staring down at his rather round belly. He kept pulling strange faces and plucked at my arm.

'I can't make my belly dance,' he complained.

'Neither can Dad,' I pointed out. 'Anyhow, I think it's women who usually do belly dancing.' (How wrong I was – as I discovered later!)

After that we got changed before we went down to supper. I had left my camera in the room and I went back for it. When I came back out I almost bumped into the Grubnoses. Mr and Mrs went striding past me, noses in the air, but Mason hung back a little. I didn't want to speak to him but he was obviously waiting for me, half blocking the corridor.

'Seen my new trainers?' boasted Mason. 'Nikes. Latest model. Cost three hundred quid.'

Oh, really? No trainers cost *that* much! Not

even when they are fluorescent orange, as Mason's were.

'Had to leave mine at home,' I said. 'Dad wouldn't let me bring them in case they got stolen. Mine cost three hundred quid – and 50p.'

Mason gave me a furious scowl. I gave him what I hoped was a charming smile.

'Your parents are pathetic,' he hissed at me. 'Your dad thinks he's funny and your mum smells.'

'Of roses,' I hastily added.

'No, stupid, she smells of a thousand-year-old toilet.'

'People didn't have toilets a thousand years ago. Not proper ones.'

'Think you're clever, don't you?' sneered Mason.

'Actually, according to my teacher I'm a little bit above average. How about you?'

Mason didn't bother to answer. 'If you sing tonight I'm going to throw tomatoes at you. I'm saving all my tomatoes from supper and I shall throw them at the whole lot of you, and your smelly mum and your smelly dad and those stupid smelly twins. So there.'

And he went stumping off after his parents. Why are some people like that? I mean, what's the point? The hotel had organized a fun evening and Mason wanted to ruin it. Why? Don't ask me.

There was a real feeling of excitement when I got to the dining room. A small space had been left in one corner and there was a little platform and a microphone for anyone who wanted to sing and enough space for a belly dancer or two.

After we had eaten, the karaoke began. Some of the singers were actually quite good, but others were so bad you wanted to run from the room and hide your ears in the pool outside. Dad sang 'I Did It My Way' and pulled funny faces and at the end he tried to sing the last verse standing on his head. I knew Dad was thinking

that was hilariously funny because, of course, he *was* singing it *his way*. Unfortunately he just looked rather daft because he kept falling over. A few people saw the funny side of it.

Mr Grubnose suddenly pushed back his chair and strode to the stage, practically pushing my dad out of the way so that he could have a go. Guess what he sang. 'Rule Britannia'! He did! He stood there and bellowed out 'Rule Britannia'. It was so awful and when he finished the audience kindly gave him a polite clap, while Mrs Grubnose got to her feet and shouted 'Hurrah! Encore!' over and over again.

Luckily the belly dancer arrived and instantly got everyone's attention. She was a rather plump lady and she was wearing an extraordinary version of a bikini that had veils of cloth hanging from it and was covered with sequins and sparkling jewels.

It turned out that it wasn't just her belly that was dancing, she also made her thighs and top half and shoulders dance too. It seemed as if she could make almost any part of her body sort of shiver and shake. It was amazingly clever and all the jewels and sequins shone and glittered as if she was wearing stars all over her.

I saw Irfan make his way to the stage and he began to dance beside her, doing the same thing. He made his shoulders and chest quiver and then his belly and then the top half of his legs. The audience were all shouting encouragement and got to their feet and cheered as the music got louder and faster and the dance moves quickened and got more and more exciting.

I was taking photos and Mum was videoing the whole thing. She moved closer to the stage and as she passed the Grubnoses' table she seemed to trip. All of a sudden Mum was hurtling towards the two dancers. She crashed into Irfan, who staggered back against the wall, arms waving like windmills as he fell over. Mum did much the same thing, and the next moment the fire alarm went off. The alarm was deafening and seconds later the sprinklers in the ceiling began to shower everyone with water. It was a deluge!

Panic! Chaos! People were screaming and rushing about in all directions. Guests came stumbling out of their rooms at the sound of the alarm and immediately stepped into an indoor rain storm.

Tomato was yelling at Mum and Dad and me.

'Bumpy will drown! Save Bumpy!'

'What's she going on about?' Dad shouted above the general noise and the din of the fire bell.

'Bumpy will drown!'

'Who on earth is Bumpy?' asked Dad.

'My tortoise!'

'What do you mean, your tortoise?'

'Bumpy! He can't swim! He'll drown. Nicky told me.' Tomato was sobbing, adding tears to the puddles that were rapidly joining up into a flood across the dining-room floor. People were splashing through them, trying to get to the exits.

Mum turned to me. Dad turned to me.

'Bumpy?' they chorused.

Oh, well. Sometimes you just have to bite the bullet and do what you have to do. 'There's a tortoise in the bath in our room. Tomato brought him back from Letoon.'

'Right, I see,' said Mum. 'But what is it doing in the bath?'

'Tomato thought it needed water to swim. I was just telling her only turtles can swim when we had to come down for supper and karaoke and everything.' I suddenly brightened up as I realized something very important. 'Anyhow, Bumpy won't drown because any water will just go down the plug hole.'

'Oh, good,' said Mum. 'I'm so glad the tortoise won't drown. However, we shall drown *if we don't get out of here. I am soaking wet!*'

Dad jerked a thumb in the right direction. 'Door's over there,' he said. But before we could escape the rain we were suddenly confronted by a purple-faced Mr Grubnose, spluttering with rage.

'I have never in my life come across anything as ridiculous as you,' he told my dad.

'Oh? You should have seen yourself singing "Rule Britannia",' Dad countered, wiping a slick of wet hair away from his eyes.

Mum jabbed him with her elbow.

'Don't answer him,' she advised. 'You'll only make yourself as bad as he is.'

'Oh, so I'm bad, am I?' demanded Mr Grubnose. 'You're the one that's bad. You set off the fire alarm and the sprinklers, you stupid woman.'

'Don't you dare call my wife a stupid woman,' shouted Dad.

'I want Bumpy,' murmured Tomato, watching the adults with worried eyes.

'Oh? So it's not stupid to set off sprinklers when there isn't even a fire?' shouted Mr Grubnose.

'It was an accident,' I put in.

Mr Grubnose's eyes bulged. Little bits of foam were forming at the sides of his mouth.

'Huh! An accident? Don't be ridiculous. First of all your father tries to stand on his head, as if that isn't silly enough, then your mother sets off the sprinklers. Your family are hooligans, hooligans and yobs.'

'Yeah,' shouted Mason from somewhere behind his father. 'Yobs!' Suddenly a large, fat, very tomato-ish tomato went whizzing past my ear and splatted on the wall behind. It was quickly followed by another tomato, which also just missed me but hit a young man on the back of his head.

'Hey! Who did that?' The young man whirled round just in time to see Mason about to launch another tomato. The man seized a cucumber from the salad table and hurled it at Mason. The cucumber went cartwheeling through the downpour and hit an old lady right between the shoulder blades.

In an instant the room was a whirling mass of vegetables criss-crossing each other, people running and shouting, some hiding under tables, others standing *on* the tables and chucking vegetables right, left and centre. And all the time

the water carried on cascading down from the ceiling. Dad grabbed hold of the twins. 'This way!' he said, finally getting us to the exit and we stepped outside into the dry just in time to watch the fire engine pull up. Out leaped six firemen, who quickly unrolled their hoses.

The Fire Chief started yelling instructions at his men and the hotel manager rushed out and shouted at the Fire Chief. I think Arif was trying to tell him there was no fire, but it was too late. They were already dashing into the hotel, hoses on full SPLURGE setting.

Dad looked at us and shrugged.

'Let's go to the beach and have an ice cream,' he suggested. So we did. The ice-cream man gave us some very peculiar looks, which wasn't surprising as we were all soaked. We sat on the beach, watched the sunset and waited for everything at the hotel to calm down.

7. The Hissing Bush

It was three hours before we were allowed back into the hotel. The dining room was still dripping with water, but the fire crew had gone and all was fairly quiet. The spray from the hoses had washed away most of the tomato splats but there were still rather a lot of mashed and squashed vegetables lying on the floor, not to mention an aubergine that had somehow got stuck to the ceiling.

Luckily there was no sign of the Grubnoses. Maybe they'd been mown down by an avalanche of tomatoes. I hoped so.

Arif, the hotel manager, apologized to all of us for what had happened and assured us that he would get to the bottom of the disaster and find out how it had started. Mum shook her head.

'I tripped on something and fell. It might have been my camera that hit the fire alarm. It was an accident. I'm so sorry,' she explained.

But the manager wouldn't hear of it. 'No, no, not your fault. It was that Irfan. I know him. He is always doing crazy things to make people laugh.' He scowled. 'He is hotel worker, not a comedian. I am always telling him. He has gone too far. Irfan is to blame. Heads must roll.'

'Oh dear,' said Mum, looking even more worried than before.

'Is Bumpy all right?' Tomato asked, squeezing my hand.

'I'm sure Bumpy's fine,' I answered.

The manager was looking at us curiously. 'Who is Bumpy?' he asked.

We all looked at each other, rather frantically. Who was going to say what?

'My tortoise!' said Tomato.

'You've got a tortoise?' asked the manager. 'In my hotel?'

'Yes, and she's –'

'Stuffed!' I interrupted.

'A stuffed tortoise?' repeated the manager.

'I mean, it's a toy tortoise. A stuffed toy.' I gave Tomato a hard stare. 'It's your favourite *toy*, isn't it, Tomato?' I kept nodding at her and smiling encouragingly.

Seconds seemed to pass. Minutes seemed to pass as I waited for Tomato to catch on. Would she? The silence continued. Tomato took a deep breath. I was still holding mine!

'Yes,' she said at last, and I started breathing again. So did Mum and Dad, but the hotel manager hadn't finished with us.

'Excuse me, but is Tomato a common name for a girl in Britain? And Cheese for a boy? It sounds very strange.'

Dad puffed up his chest proudly. 'These are the only twins in the world called Cheese and Tomato.'

'But why give them such strange names?' asked Arif.

'They were born in the back of a pizza delivery van,' Dad explained, as if that made it all perfectly clear and OK.

The manager's eyebrows slid up his forehead. 'Oh,' he murmured, and Mum could see that he was struggling with the idea, trying to make sense of it all. She quickly brought the matter to a close.

'Come on, upstairs, all of you. It's bedtime.'

So we all said good night to Arif and left him at the bottom of the stairs with his eyebrows still stuck at the top of his head.

'It's about time we sorted out this nonsense about tortoises,' said Mum as we went into our room.

Well, of course Mum soon discovered it wasn't nonsense at all. There was Bumpy, living proof, still plodding up and down the bath and occasionally staring at the plug hole as if it might be an escape tunnel if only he could fit into it.

'Good grief!' cried Mum, and then she began laughing. 'He's quite big, isn't he? How on earth did the twins manage to bring a tortoise back from Letoon? We never noticed anything. Did you know about this, Nicholas?'

I shook my head. 'Not until Tomato showed

me when we got back to the hotel. It was a bit late by then and I thought it was safer for the tortoise to stay in the bath than taking him back outside and dumping him.'

'Hmm.' Mum paused and thought. 'First thing tomorrow we must take Bumpy – as you call him – out to a wild patch and let him go.'

'Nooo!' squeaked Tomato, her face collapsing and her bottom lip suggesting that a flood of tears was imminent.

Mum crouched down to hug her. 'Darling, this is a wild tortoise. It's not like Schumacher, our tortoise at home. Schumacher has been with us since he was a baby. He's a pet. Bumpy is a wild tortoise who likes to explore and meet other wild tortoises. Making Bumpy into a pet would be like putting him in prison. We have to let him go.'

Tomato sniffed. Cheese peered over the edge of the bath.

'Shall I put the lettuce back then?' he asked.

Mum was mystified. 'What lettuce?' she asked.

Cheese began to pull a great wodge of lettuce leaves out of his pocket.

'Where on earth did that lot come from?' asked Mum.

Cheese looked at me. 'There were some on the table downstairs and Nicky said we needed to feed Bumpy so I got some.'

Mum sighed and rubbed her forehead. 'Leave it in the bath for now,' she said. 'Then he'll be able to find it if he wants something to eat.'

What an exhausting evening! There was one strange thing I noticed before I went to bed. I had slipped downstairs to check on the kittens. As I went past Reception I saw the Grubnoses talking to the hotel manager and Irfan. The

Grubnoses were scowling at Irfan, and Arif, the manager, was wearing a very serious face while Irfan appeared not to understand what the problem was. I tried to catch Irfan's eye so he could see I was going to look at the kittens but he was too taken up with whatever little drama was taking place with the Grubnoses. When I headed back upstairs to bed they had all vanished.

We didn't see Irfan at breakfast. It was unlike him not to be there. The dining room was still closed and we sat at tables outside, in the sunshine, which was lovely. Turkish breakfasts are the best!

There weren't all that many guests eating breakfast, which was a little strange. Usually it is a really busy time. We also missed Irfan, who always chatted with us and made us laugh.

We were halfway through breakfast when I heard a nearby bush hiss at me. My first thought was that it was a snake, but it didn't sound quite right. The hissing was quite regular too.

'Psssst! Psssst! Psssst!'

It was definitely coming from the bush. I looked at it carefully. Suddenly some of the branches parted and a face appeared.

'Irfan! What are you doing?' I whispered, and by this time the rest of the family had noticed too.

'I'm hiding in bush,' said Irfan, which was perfectly obvious.

'I can see that. Why?'

'I have no job!' he answered and he drew his finger across his throat. 'Manager say all my fault.

Lots of guests have left hotel and gone to a different one. All because of water, tomatoes, mess, fire – all my fault. Manager says.'

'But it wasn't anything to do with you!' I exclaimed.

'I know. But Mr Manager, Arif, he wants to blame someone. He doesn't like me because always happy. Me always happy. Him always grimpy.'

'Grumpy?' I suggested, and Irfan smiled.

'Yes, grumpy. Now Arif blame me and I have no job.'

'Oh, Irfan, I'm so sorry,' said Mum. 'I think it was my fault. I told the manager, but he said someone else was to blame. I'm so, so sorry,' she repeated.

'Some people told manager it was me,' Irfan said quietly.

'No! Who?' cried Mum. 'Who would do such a thing?'

I knew. Dad knew. I think Mum knew too.

The Grubnoses. Of course – that was what they were up to last night.

Irfan shrugged. 'What can I do? I can't say anything. Mr Manager has decided. He won't listen.'

Dad was quietly growling to himself, like an angry tiger. Now he leaned forward, closer to Irfan.

'Listen to me, Irfan. We will sort this. We will get your job back. I don't know how, but we shall. Keep in touch with us so we can tell you what is going on.'

'*Tamam*. OK.' Irfan nodded. 'I still have friends in hotel. They will tell me too. You are my friends too.'

'Of course we are!' I said, while Cheese and Tomato suddenly got off their chairs, rushed across to the bush and started hugging it. At least it looked like they were hugging the bush. One or two people saw them and wondered what was going on but didn't say anything.

Dad got up. 'I'm going to have words with the manager right now,' he said.

'I'm coming too,' said Mum. 'The fire alarm going off was my fault. I won't have the manager blaming you, Irfan. Nicholas, keep an eye on Cheese and Tomato, OK?'

I nodded and watched Mum and Dad head off to the manager's office. As soon as they were inside the hotel Irfan spoke to us again.

'You remember kittens I showed you?'

'They're so SWEEEET!' squeaked Tomato.

'I'm not in hotel now, so I can't look after them. Maybe –'

'– WE CAN!' shouted Cheese.

'Sssh,' said Irfan. 'No one must know. You bring them to me and I will take them.'

'We'll get them,' said Cheese, so I gave him my keycard for the door. Cheese pulled at his sister. 'Come on. I've got an idea.'

The twins disappeared. I wasn't sure if I should go after them but I was certain they would be

OK with the kittens and it gave them something to do.

Five minutes later they were back, with no kittens. Instead they handed Bumpy the tortoise to Irfan. I quickly explained about how we ended up with a tortoise.

'She's wild,' Tomato told Irfan seriously. 'And she has to go to a wild place.'

'But where are the kittens?' asked Irfan, rather bewildered by all this animal swapping.

'In our bedroom, in the bath!' Cheese announced triumphantly. 'We're going to look after them instead of the tortoise and take them home on the plane and they will live with us forever and ever!'

8. The Big Splash

Mum and Dad didn't get anywhere with the hotel manager. Arif was convinced that Irfan had caused the trouble that led to all the damage and the ruined evening. It was true that several guests had already left for other hotels. Arif was losing business and was not a happy man.

In the meantime I had found a small basket for the kittens and settled them down under my bed where they couldn't be seen.

Now we were all sitting round the hotel pool, at least Mum and Dad and I were lounging while Cheese and Tomato splashed about in the shallow end, wearing their arm bands and generally trying to drown each other. (Just joking!)

We had also been joined by Ice Cream. That dog hung around outside the hotel *all* the time, waiting for us to appear. Then she would cheerfully follow us wherever we went. She seemed to think she belonged to us, or maybe it was the other way round, and we belonged to her. Somehow she had managed to get into the hotel's back garden, where the pool was, and now she was sunbathing, spreadeagled next to Dad's chair.

Across the pool on the far side I could see the Grubnoses watching the twins as if they were

some kind of low life, like giant slugs that should be quickly sprayed with something terribly shrivelling.

'So, just how are we going to get Irfan's job back?' Mum asked Dad, her eyebrows raised.

'I shall think of something.' Dad sat back in his chair and closed his eyes. 'Now let me cogitate in peace,' he murmured.

Mum looked at me and rolled her eyes. 'Cogitate? That's a big word for a small brain! What's the betting he'll start snoring any moment?'

Two minutes later it began

SNNNNNNRRRRRRRRRRRR!

'Told you so,' said Mum. She didn't see Dad open one eye and wink at me. I winked back and we left him to his cogitations. Over on the far side of the pool I saw Mason scowling at me. He pretended to pull a pin from a hand grenade and chuck it in my direction. Charming!

The twins were getting noisier. They were

chasing each other right round the pool and then they would hurl themselves into the water, laughing and giggling and trying to make the biggest splash.

Mr Grubnose suddenly put down his book and got to his feet.

'Can't you control those two monsters of yours?' he bellowed across at us. He pointed at a notice in Turkish at one end of the pool. 'You do understand what that notice says? It says NO JUMPING IN THE POOL. SPLASHING IS FORBIDDEN.'

Dad was woken by the shouting. He sat up. 'It's in Turkish,' he shouted back at Mr Grubnose. 'They can't read Turkish. Leave them alone. They're just enjoying themselves.'

'*WOOF! WOOF! GRRURRFFF! FFFFFF! WOOOOFF!*' went Ice Cream, now on her feet and baring her teeth at the noisy man on the other side of the pool.

Dad laughed. 'You tell him, Ice Cream!'

Mr Grubnose waved a fist, sat down in a huff and snatched up his book.

(Much later on, Irfan told us that the sign didn't say anything about jumping at all. It just said: ATTENTION! SHARKS IN THE POOL! Irfan had made it and put up the sign himself, as a joke.)

The twins carried on chasing each other and splashing about. Ice Cream thought it all looked like a lot of fun and trotted over. She barked at them cheerfully and followed them round and round, trotting after them with her tail held high and wagging madly. Then Tomato jumped in the pool and Ice Cream followed, landing with a big splash and madly doing the doggy paddle across to her.

Cheese squeaked with delight and went for the biggest splash ever. He leaped high into the air and a moment later he came thumping down into the water.

SPER-LASHHHHH!

SHWOOOOOooSH!

A gigantic cascade of water sprayed up over the side, engulfing all three Grubnoses.

That was it. They were *furious*! I thought all their heads would come shooting off their necks they were so mad. Even Mason was hopping about as if his fabulously expensive orange trainers were on fire – which was impossible since they were soaking wet. Ha, ha!

I can't tell you exactly what they said because there were some bad words involved. They went on and on about pool rules and no dogs and disgusting children and hooligan families and a dreadful hotel and this shouldn't be permitted and that shouldn't be permitted. I ended up thinking it's amazing we were actually allowed to breathe.

The Grubnoses went storming off to speak to the hotel manager and the next thing was Arif came striding angrily across to us to let us know that the Grubnoses had left the hotel to go somewhere better and more peaceful and it was all *our* fault.

Oh dear. (And the manager doesn't even know

about the three kittens in the bedroom, yet!) Arif yelled at Ice Cream and aimed a few kicks at her (which all missed), driving her out of the garden and back on to the street.

Cheese and Tomato stood beside the pool and watched in horror. I tried to comfort them.

'Don't worry. She'll be back. She won't have gone far.'

'Bad man!' said Tomato.

'Poo man!' muttered Cheese.

'Arif is just doing his job,' I told them. 'After all, this is his hotel. Some of the guests don't like cats and dogs. The manager has to deal with that.'

'Why don't they like cats and dogs?' asked Tomato.

'Some people don't. Maybe they've met a bad dog. Maybe they've been bitten by a dog. Then they might think most dogs are like that and they want to feel safe so they won't go near them.'

'Cats don't bite,' said Cheese.

'Yes, they do, and they scratch too.'

'They don't scratch everyone,' Tomato put in.

'No, not everyone,' I agreed.

'Only bad people,' Tomato added.

'I don't think it's as simple as that,' I began, but Tomato was already formulating her plan.

'So, so, so the scratchy people can go somewhere else and the un-scratchy people can come here and the kittens won't scratch them. They'll just *prrr-prrr miaow* and say hello.'

Tomato seemed very satisfied with her solution to the problem and carried on. 'And the bited people can go somewhere else too and the un-bited people can come here and Ice Cream can go swimming with us again.'

I sighed. 'I suppose so. Anyhow, you say "bitten", not "bited".' But Tomato wasn't interested in that. She had sorted out the world of cats and dogs and hotels and that was all that mattered.

Unfortunately Tomato also wasn't interested in solving the problem of how Irfan could get his job back. That was what Mum and Dad and I were trying to sort out. Well, Dad had actually gone back to snoring so that just left Mum and me.

This was Mum's idea.

And this was my idea.

So, as you can see, none of us was doing very well.

9. Wardrobes and a Very Scrappy Plan

Did I tell you that Ice Cream is in our room now? Well, she is. I'm not sure when it happened, but I do know that it couldn't have happened without someone (or some-two!) helping her. I'm sure you can guess who the some-two were.

The twins are certain that keeping the animals in our room will convince Mum and Dad to take them all home with us. They are going to be hugely disappointed, but I'm too soft to tell them right now. Or maybe I'm just a bit of a coward when it comes to delivering BAD NEWS.

How can we possibly take them home? We can't smuggle them on to the plane. All the baggage goes through the detector machines at the airport. So do we! The animals will be taken away from us and that will cause a major scene, with Tomato and Cheese probably screaming the place down. On the other hand, if I take the animals away from Cheese and Tomato now, they'll scream the hotel down!

Besides, I have to share a room with them. They will probably never speak to me again if I tell them the animals have to stay behind – not to mention the fact that they shouldn't be in the bedroom.

In the meantime, Ice Cream has taken up a completely relaxed 'this-is-my-home' position on the double bed that they share. I know Mum and Dad play along with the twins and pretend that Ice Cream is 'their' dog. What Mum and Dad don't realize is that the twins aren't playing at all. They really think that Ice Cream is *their* dog and she is going home with them.

Our room has turned into an animal rescue centre! They all look very pleased with themselves too, and when I say 'they' I mean the

three kittens, Ice Cream *and* the twins.

By this morning my brain was beginning to ache with all these problems. As if I didn't have enough to think about, it was clear from the noises the kittens were making that they were hungry. Then Ice Cream made one or two tongue-slapping grunts that suggested a nice little snack would go down very well.

None of us had any money for food. Irfan was nowhere to be seen. (I checked in all the bushes!) Where could I find food? The answer was obvious, really. Where do you find food in a hotel? In the kitchen. And the kitchen was bound to have a waste bin. It might even be *outside* the kitchen, which would help a lot.

I left the twins to keep an eye on the animals and went downstairs to spy out the land. I walked casually past the kitchen a few times, peering in through the open door. Then I took a look from the outside.

The good news was that there was a bin for scraps. The bad news was that it was inside the kitchen. It was close to the back door, but it was still going to be awkward to get at. The kitchen staff would certainly see me. Then it came to me – my BIG IDEA. If I could get the kitchen staff out of the way, then I could nip in, grab some scraps and disappear, like a phantom in the night. (Except that it would be broad daylight and I'm not at all ghostly.)

All I needed was something to distract the staff and hopefully get all four of them out of the kitchen for a minute or two. And the answer to that problem was lying on a double bed in my very own room upstairs.

ICE CREAM!

I raced back upstairs, sat Cheese and Tomato down on one of the beds and told them about the plan. I was going to need their help to pull it off. They thought it was brilliant, which was very satisfying until they got completely over-excited and started jumping on the beds and tearing round the room. That set off Ice Cream, barking like mad. I hastily clamped her mouth shut and she looked at me with her eyebrows waggling up and down with surprise. It was going to be important to keep her quiet, at least for the time being.

I looped one of my belts round Ice Cream's neck a couple of times to make a collar, so we could hold on to her. We crept down to the kitchen, where there was a great clattering of pans, taps gushing water, cooks shouting at each other and lots of very busy noises in general.

Ice Cream kept tugging at her collar. She could smell food and she was hungry. She began to growl.

'Sssh! Quiet! Just be patient, will you?' I hissed. She waggled her eyebrows at me again, but went quiet. I peered round the edge of the kitchen door. This was it – time to put my plan into action.

'OK. Are you two ready?'

The twins nodded and grinned.

'Cheese and Tomato, you stay here and get ready to grab Ice Cream. Once you have her, go straight back to our bedroom as fast as possible and wait for me to come up with the food. Got that?'

They nodded, made 'Shush!' and 'You shush first!' noises at each other and then stood like sentries on either side of the kitchen door.

I took Ice Cream and hurried round to the back door. Ice Cream was already straining at her collar, wanting to get at all the food. Good!

I let her go.

Ice Cream went charging in. There was a moment of uncanny silence and then the dog-bomb went off. Boom!

'DOG! DOG IN THE KITCHEN!' someone yelled. (In Turkish!) Pans were dropped. People screamed, yelled and generally made an awful lot

of noise. I peered inside. The staff were rushing about as if they were in some crazy comedy film! Some were chasing the dog. One had climbed on to a table and had his apron over his face as if that meant the dog couldn't see him.

'GET THE DOG!' bellowed the head chef, hurling a large saucepan *and* his hat in Ice Cream's direction. (They both missed.)

All that fuss, just because of a small dog! Ice Cream was brilliant. It was almost as if she understood exactly what I wanted her to do. She waited until all the staff were after her and then went skidding off to the kitchen door, where Cheese and Tomato were ready to spirit her away.

I waited until everyone was out of the kitchen and then took advantage of the chaos and dashed in. I rifled through the scraps bin. URGH! But it had to be done. I filled my carrier bag with as much meaty food as I could find, then raced back out. Once outside, I walked in a more sensible and normal manner back to our room. I didn't want to draw attention to myself. Luckily nobody noticed that I had bits of manky vegetable from the scraps bin stuck halfway up one arm.

We met back in our room. This time we *all* jumped on the beds! It had gone brilliantly well. Cheese and Tomato were cheering. Ice Cream was barking.

That was when there was a loud noise at the door. *KNOCK! KERNOCK!*

We froze. I grabbed Ice Cream, clamped my hand round her muzzle to keep her quiet and climbed into the wardrobe. Tomato closed the door on me. There was a tiny gap between the doors where I could just about see into the room.

'Come on,' said Dad, knocking on the bedroom door again. 'Open up!'

Cheese slowly opened the door.

'What was all that noise?' asked Dad. 'I heard barking. Is there a dog in here?'

'No.' Tomato shook her head. After all, she wasn't exactly lying. She hadn't got a dog in *there*.

I had the dog *here* in the wardrobe!

'Where's Nicholas? I thought he was with you?'

'He went,' said Cheese.

'Went where?' Dad asked.

Cheese shrugged. I could see him pointing nervously around the room and eventually jabbing a finger straight at my wardrobe.

No, Cheese! Not the wardrobe! Noooooooo!

Dad stared straight at me. At least that's what it seemed like.

'Oh, ha ha,' said Dad. 'Very funny. Good joke. I expect he went downstairs, did he?'

'Yes,' Tomato said quickly, thank goodness.

'Right,' said Dad, looking around. 'You'd better tidy up before your mother comes in here. This room is in a right mess. Anyone would think you were keeping a zoo up here. Do a bit of tidying, please?'

'OK,' chorused the twins, as Dad left.

Cheese opened the wardrobe door. 'You can come out now,' he told me.

'Why did you tell Dad where I was?' I demanded.

'Because that *is* where you was,' said Cheese.

'Where he were,' corrected Tomato, getting her grammar wrong too.

'But –' I began, and then realized there wasn't any point in trying to explain it all to a three-year-old. The important thing was that we had all escaped, including Ice Cream.

We hauled the little kitty basket out from beneath my bed, gave them some food and gave some to Ice Cream too. We had at least solved that problem.

But what about Irfan's job?

10. Those Orange Trainers Should Be Arrested!

Cracking morning! Mum came rushing into our room. She was very excited and waved her video camera at me.

'I think we can prove Irfan had nothing to do with the fire alarm,' she said. 'I was afraid the camera had been damaged when I smashed it into the alarm, not to mention all that water spraying all over the place – but it's fine. It's still working properly. Anyhow, I was checking to see what had been filmed. Take a look at this.'

I peered at the little screen on the side of the camera. It started with Dad's karaoke.

'Hang on, you don't want that,' said Mum with a shudder, pressing the fast-forward button. 'Ah, this is where it starts. Look.'

The belly dancing had begun. Mum had been sitting at our table when she started filming. The scene jiggled a bit as she got to her feet and carried on wobbling as she made her way to the front for a better view. Suddenly the film jerked all over the place. As Mum tripped on something the film showed a flash of ceiling, wall, people, her own feet, a blur of orange, the floor, yet more ceiling, a glimpse of red and then – nothing. The film had stopped.

But, the important bit was when Mum tripped, because the camera showed clearly that she didn't exactly trip. *She was tripped up by someone's foot!*

I recognized that foot at once because it was wearing a bright orange, very expensive Nike trainer. Mason! He had deliberately tripped up

my mother! Not only that but after that moment the film scrabbled about madly and suddenly went all blurred until *BAMM!* The camera smashed into something red and stopped.

'Watch carefully, Nicholas,' said Mum, rewinding the film. She showed the end in slow motion. It was still blurry until moments before the finish, when it all came into focus and yes, there was the fire alarm and, *BAMM!*, the camera hit the fire alarm.

I punched the air. 'That's brilliant! The manager can't possibly say it was Irfan's fault. This proves it was the camera that hit the fire alarm *and* it wasn't even an accident, because that snotty Mason Grubnose deliberately tripped you up. He and his orange trainers should be arrested!'

'Exactly. Your father and I are going to take this down to Arif straight away. The holiday ends tomorrow, so there's not much time left for us to sort things out. In fact you and the twins should start packing. We've an early start tomorrow.'

That left me rather open-mouthed. Packing to go? Already? So much had been going on I had lost track of time. Our bit of fun with the pets in our room would have to end.

Oh dear.

Even as Mum left the room to go to meet the manager I could see the twins looking at me. Tomato's lower lip was already quivering. I felt that it wouldn't be long before mine was too. This was going to be heartbreaking for all of us, especially Ice Cream, who thought we were her family.

'I'm sorry,' I said. 'What can I do? We have to let the animals go back on the street. We've had lots of fun with them, but now we have to say goodbye.'

'They'll DIE!' wailed Cheese. 'It's all your fault! They'll be deaded!'

'We'll stop you!' shouted Tomato.

'Look, I don't want this to happen either, but it's like I said right at the beginning – we can't take them home on the plane. We really, really can't. It's not allowed.'

'We'll hide them.'

'No, you won't. Do you remember the scanners at the airport? Do you remember seeing some people having their luggage searched? You won't be able to get the animals past the scanners. The airport security police will take the animals from us and put them in cages or just dump them outside. Now, do you want the animals to be let out on the streets they know here, or would you rather they were dumped miles away at the airport?'

Tomato gave me her if-you-touch-those-animals-I-will-eat-your-legs look.

'It's got to be done,' I repeated. I pulled the

basket of kitties out from beneath my bed. I had to lie down to do this, of course, and in an instant the twins had pounced on me. I found myself trying to shake off two squealing, squawking, three-year-old hyenas while carefully carrying a basket of kittens. I managed to get to my feet with Tomato clamped to my left leg and Cheese clamped to the right.

I struggled to the door, calling Ice Cream. Like the lovely, wonderful, good dog she was, she came trotting after me. Out into the corridor we went, with Cheese and Tomato yelling and me trying to go down the stairs balancing a basket of kittens, with the twins clamped to each leg.

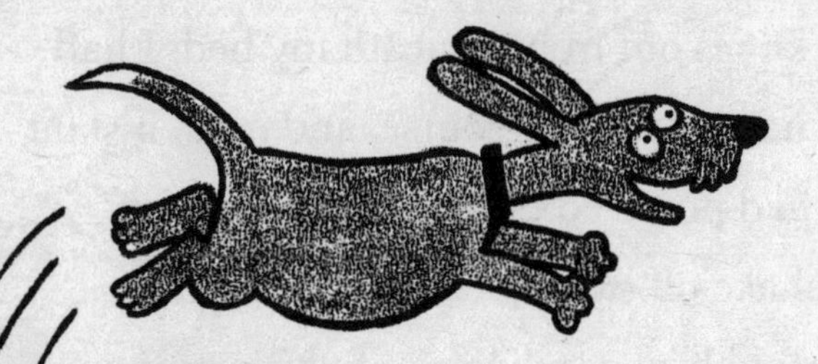

I'm sure Tomato was trying to eat my knees.

I had almost reached the open door to the street when Cheese suddenly threw himself in front of me. I almost went flying, trying to avoid stepping on him. The basket lurched from my hands. The kittens meowed and spat as they hit the floor and immediately went scampering off in three different directions. Ice Cream chased after one, then the other, then another, but she might just as well have chased her own tail.

All the noise attracted the other street dogs and two of them came bursting into the hotel lobby to see what all the fun was. They were closely followed by about ten more. I lost count. Dogs of every shape and size were all over the place, barking furiously.

The manager came hurrying out of his little office, followed by my parents, and immediately got mown down by three kittens being chased by an avalanche of dogs.

'Save them, Mummy!' cried Cheese, snot dribbling down his face from all his tears.

Tomato was sitting on a step sobbing.

That was when Irfan arrived.

'Hey! Hey!' he shouted, clapping his hands. 'Go on, out!'

The street dogs suddenly stopped, looked at him, turned tail and ran. It was astonishing. It was as if Irfan was Doctor Dolittle or something. As the dogs retreated Cheese and Tomato ran around the room gathering up the kittens into their arms. As for Ice Cream, when Irfan arrived the dog simply went across to Mum and sat quietly at her feet.

The manager heaved a huge sigh of relief as the last dog vanished.

'How did you *do* that?' Arif asked Irfan.

'All the street dogs know me, and the street cats. I feed them. I talk to them. They are my friends.' He studied Arif's face. 'Sometimes I think animals are better than people. More friendly.'

Arif smiled and clapped Irfan on the shoulder. 'You are a strange man, Irfan. I don't understand you, but I can see you are a good man.' Arif glanced at us. 'These kind people have shown me a film. I was wrong. It wasn't you that caused the sprinkler to go off. Madam was right. It was her, but it was an accident caused by a boy.'

That was news to Irfan. He was very surprised. 'A boy?' He looked at me in surprise. I quickly shook my head.

The manager nodded and looked very serious. 'Mason Grubnose. I think his family will have to pay for some of the damage. But, more importantly, if you will forgive me, you can come back to work here. The guests like you. I don't know why, but they do!'

They laughed and shook hands. Irfan had his job. The smile on his face was something to treasure. Now he looked at Cheese and Tomato. He wanted to know what had been going on. I told him everything. It was Mum and Dad's turn to be surprised.

'You mean you really did have a zoo in the bedroom?' Dad asked incredulously.

'Not exactly a zoo, Dad,' I pointed out. 'Just three kittens and Ice Cream. I did tell the twins several times we couldn't possibly take them home on the plane.'

'Oh, but you can.'

! ? ! ? ! ? ! ? ! ? ! ? ! ? !

We all turned and looked at Irfan, gobsmacked.

11. Centipedes as Big as Elephants

'It's true,' Irfan said. 'I am part of an animal-rescue group. Why do all the street dogs of Kalkan look so healthy and happy? Because KAPSA looks after them. KAPSA stands for **K**alkan **A**ssociation for the **P**rotection of **S**treet **A**nimals.'

Dad screwed up his face. 'Just a moment. That would be K-A-F-T-P-O-S-A,' he said, sounding it out. 'KAFTPOSA, not KAPSA.'

Mum nudged him hard. 'Stop it, Ron! Do go on, Irfan.'

'I know KAPSA,' Arif put in eagerly. 'One of the people who helped start it is an Englishwoman, Maggie. She lives here. I know her. She has a shop. I bought some jeans from her. Very expensive. Turkish jeans much cheaper.

But these designer jeans. I like Maggie. She has so many dogs, cats too. KAPSA do good work. Kalkan dogs and cats look nice now, not all boney-boney.'

Irfan nodded. 'Tourists come, fall in love with a stray dog or cat and ask if the animal can go to their country with them. We give them the right injections and travel documents and send them – sixty-one animals this year already.' He grinned proudly. 'You can take animals home, if you want.'

The twins did want! So did I. But what about Mum and Dad?

Dad was shaking his head. 'We can't do that, can we? I mean, we've already got a small zoo. There's Schumacher the tortoise, Rubbish the goat, all the hens and rabbits, loads of spiders, woodlice, earthworms, earwigs, ants, bugs of all kinds.' Dad began to nod, pulling at his beard. 'Centipedes!' he added suddenly, as if centipedes as big as elephants were stomping about all over our garden. 'Yep, it's pretty full back there.'

Ice Cream got to her feet, padded across to Dad, leaned gently against Dad's legs and looked up at him. Ice Cream's eyes didn't go all soft and gooey and pleading as you might expect. She simply looked up at Dad and her eyes were asking a very intelligent question (for a dog!). *What are you going to do, big man? Are you going to leave me behind or are you going to take me?*

Irfan's eyes were on Dad too.

Mum bent down and stroked Ice Cream's head. 'She *is* a lovely dog,' she murmured and as she spoke Ice Cream rested one of her front paws on Mum's foot as if she was trying to hold hands with her.

Even the twins had become silent, waiting to hear what Dad would say.

'I think –' Dad began, and Ice Cream shifted her paw to Dad's foot and nudged her nose against Dad's leg.

'I think –' Dad repeated, wrestling with his own mind.

Ice Cream was losing patience. She began to growl. She clamped her jaws round Dad's ankle and gently chewed at it, growling softly. *Come on, make up your mind!*

'Oh, OK, then,' Dad growled back, trying to shake Ice Cream off the end of his leg.

Talk about wild cheering! And dancing! And running around madly! Not to mention Ice

Cream jumping and barking and Irfan and the manager laughing and Mum happily crying and everyone patting the dog and Ice Cream looking as if she'd just eaten every ice cream from the ice-cream shop.

Just at that crazy, happy moment who should come strolling past – the Grubnoses.

'Don't look, Mason,' said Mrs Grubnose in a loud voice. 'It's that horrible family and they've got one of those nasty street dogs with them. Just walk past quietly and don't look.'

'Ah!' cried Arif. 'Mr and Mrs Grubnose! The very people I would like to see. You seem to have made a mistake when you told me Irfan had started all the trouble at Hotel Kismet. We have proof, on camera, film! It shows how your son, Mason, deliberately tripped this lady here and that started the trouble. All that water and damage! It was your son's fault. Please, come to my office so I can tell you how much you must pay me.'

Have you ever seen someone's suntan disappear in a few seconds and be replaced by ghostly skin? That is what happened to all three of the Grubnoses. Then Mr Grubnose took control.

'Oh, no,' he said sternly. 'I know what you people are like. You're just trying to get someone to pay for the damage caused by your own staff. I'm not putting up with that!'

'Please, my office,' insisted the manager. But Mr Grubnose ignored him and turned to his wife and son.

'Come on, follow me. We'll have none of this.'

The family began to walk off at a brisk pace, but they hadn't reckoned with Ice Cream. She shot out from behind Dad's legs, raced after the Grubnoses, overtook them, then smartly turned, braced her legs, bared her fangs and snarled.

'Urrh!' shuddered Mrs Grubnose, clutching at Mason. 'The dog, the dog! It wants to eat us! It's probably got rabies! And Chinese rabbit pox, or something ghastly!'

Ice Cream moved towards the Grubnoses. They began to back away and bit by bit Ice Cream rounded them up and pushed them back like sheep, all the way into the manager's office.

Arif grinned at us, walked in to join them and shut the door.

I could swear Ice Cream was smiling as she came trotting back to us and sat down on the pavement.

*

And so our holiday in Turkey ended. We are home now and it will be a month or two before Ice Cream gets here. We can't wait. Maggie and Irfan send us messages and photos from time to time, to keep in touch and show us how well Ice Cream is doing with her injections and stuff.

We did have one more little problem on the way home. After all, wherever we go we always have Captain Disaster travelling with us.

It was when we were actually climbing up the steps into the plane to fly back to Britain. Dad suddenly stopped.

'Oh, no! No!'

'What's the matter?' asked Mum, thinking something awful must have happened.

'I've left my paddleboard behind,' gasped Dad. 'My paddleboard!'

Mum gave him a big smile and an equally big kiss.

'Thank goodness for that,' she said, and got into the plane. We quickly followed her and Dad, and the plane door was shut behind us.

Not Quite the End

You are probably wondering what happened to the three kittens. They found a good home. It wasn't with Irfan. It was with Arif, the manager of Hotel Kismet. He decided to keep them in the hotel and new guests would often find one, or the other, or all three, sleeping on their chair at the breakfast table and even, on the odd occasion, curled up neatly on their bed.

Jeremy Strong once worked in a bakery, putting the jam into three thousand doughnuts every night. Now he puts the jam in stories instead, which he finds much more exciting. At the age of three, he fell out of a first-floor bedroom window and landed on his head. His mother says that this damaged him for the rest of his life and refuses to take any responsibility. He loves writing stories because he says it is 'the only time you alone have complete control and can make anything happen'. His ambition is to make you laugh (or at least snuffle). Jeremy Strong lives near Bath with his wife, Gillie, three cats and a flying cow.

www.jeremystrong.co.uk

Author's Note

My wife Gillie and I have been visiting Kalkan for several years. KAPSA provides street dogs and cats with food and veterinary care and has an impressive neutering and education programme that reaches out to the surrounding villages and arranges transfers of homeless dogs and cats to new homes all over Europe. Tourists frequently arrive in Kalkan and fall in love with a certain dog or cat and decide to give it a new home. If you would like to know more about the work of KAPSA, please go to:

kapsaonline.com